Dear mouse friends,
Welcome to the world of

Geronimo Stilton

The Editorial Staff of
The Rodent's Gazette

1. Linda Thinslice
2. Sweetie Cheesetriangle
3. Ratella Redfur
4. Soya Mousehao
5. Cheesita de la Pampa
6. Coco Chocamouse
7. Mouseanna Mousetti
8. Patty Plumprat
9. Tina Spicytail
10. William Shortpaws
11. Valerie Vole
12. Trap Stilton
13. Dolly Fastpaws
14. Zeppola Zap
15. Merenguita Gingermouse
16. Shorty Tao
17. Baby Tao
18. Gigi Gogo
19. Teddy von Muffler
20. Thea Stilton
21. Erronea Misprint
22. Pinky Pick
23. Ya-ya O'Cheddar
24. Ratsy O'Shea
25. Geronimo Stilton
26. Benjamin Stilton
27. Briette Finerat
28. Raclette Finerat
29. Mousella MacMouser
30. Kreamy O'Cheddar
31. Blasco Tabasco
32. Toffie Sugarsweet
33. Tylerat Truemouse
34. Larry Keys
35. Michael Mouse

Geronimo Stilton
A learned and brainy
mouse; editor of
The Rodent's Gazette

Thea Stilton
Geronimo's sister and
special correspondent at
The Rodent's Gazette

Trap Stilton
An awful joker;
Geronimo's cousin and
owner of the store
Cheap Junk for Less

Benjamin Stilton
A sweet and loving
nine-year-old mouse;
Geronimo's favorite
nephew

Geronimo Stilton

SURF'S UP, GERONIMO!

Scholastic Inc.

New York   Toronto   London   Auckland   Sydney
Mexico City   New Delhi   Hong Kong   Buenos Aires

No part of this publication may be reproduced, stored in a retrieval system, or transmitted in any form or by any means, electronic, mechanical, photocopying, recording, or otherwise, without written permission of the publisher. For information regarding permission, write to Scholastic Inc., Attention: Permissions Department, 557 Broadway, New York, NY 10012.

ISBN-13: 978-0-439-69143-7
ISBN-10: 0-439-69143-5

Text by Geronimo Stilton
Original title: *L'hai voluta la vacanza, Stilton?*
Cover by Larry Keys
Illustrations by Larry Keys and Toprika Topraska
Graphics by Merenguita Gingermouse

Special thanks to Kathryn Cristaldi
Interior design by Kay Petronio

20 19 18 17 16   11 12/0

Printed in the U.S.A.   40
First printing, June 2005

HAVE I EVER GIVEN YOU BAD ADVICE?

Blue skies . . . sandy beaches . . . . I was dreaming of taking a vacation. Yes, I needed to escape the RAT RACE. I had been working so hard running the newspaper.

Oops, how rude. I almost forgot to introduce myself. My name is Stilton, *Geronimo Stilton*. I am the publisher of *The Rodent's Gazette*. It's the most popular paper on Mouse Island.

I love running the paper. But it is a lot of **work**. And all work and no play can

I was dreaming of taking a vacation.

make a mouse **very cranky**.
At least that's what my great-uncle Happy
Paws used to tell me. Anyway, one morning,
I passed by some travel agencies on my way
to the office. The pictures in the windows
looked so relaxing. Palm trees, cheese
bars by the pool...

I sighed. Yes, it was time to take a break.

I pushed open the door to Kick Up Your Paws. It's one of the best-known travel agencies in New Mouse City. But before I could step inside, someone pulled my tail.

"Why hello there, **Cousinkins!**" a voice screeched in my ear. "Going on vacation?"

Rats! It was my obnoxious cousin Trap. Now I definitely needed to get away.

That mouse can really get under my fur.

"Today must be your lucky day, **Geronimoid**," my cousin smirked. "I know exactly the *right* agency for **YOU**,"

He put his paw on my shoulder. "Have I ever given you bad advice?"

I chewed my whiskers. One thing you should know about Trap, he's the most untrustworthy mouse on the block!

TRUST ME, YOU'LL LIKE IT!

Two seconds later, my cousin whipped out his cell phone.

"SMOOTHIE? TRAP HERE. HOW'S IT SQUEAKING?"

he shouted into the receiver. "Scrape the cheese out of your ears, my friend. I'm

bringing over my cousin Geronimo Stilton. He's looking for a *little vacation*." He paused to pick his nose, then continued. "No, he's nothing like me, Smoothie," he chuckled. "He's not into anything exciting. No SHARK fishing. No ROCK climbing. He's a total scaredy mouse. Yeah, a real TAIL TWIRLER. You know the type. He needs a *little-old-lady* vacation. Nothing more dangerous than some sunburned fur. Ha-ha. But he's got lots of money, so don't worry about the dough. The sky's the limit with this one!"

He switched off his phone and started to scamper away.

I could not believe the **NERVE** of my cousin. How dare he? I ran after him. I was fuming. "Are you NUTS?" I cried.

"First of all, I am not a scaredy mouse. And second of all, I am not made of *money*."

Trap **rolled** his eyes.

"Well, isn't that just like you, Germeister," he muttered. "Such a PeNNY PiNChER. And so ungrateful!"

I was about to tell him I didn't need his help when I realized he'd stopped. We had arrived. We were in a *DARK ALLEY*,

far from New Mouse City's main streets. And we were standing in front of the **SHABBIEST-LOOKING** travel agency I'd ever seen.

A sign above the window read:

Through the window, I spotted a **SLEAZY-LOOKING** rodent. His paws rested on his desk. I groaned. Something told me I wasn't going to like it. No, I had a feeling I wasn't going to like it one bit!

I spotted a sleazy-looking rodent.

HELLO, GERATTIMO?

The mouse snickered when we came through the door. I wondered what was so funny. Then I stared at his outfit. Now *there* was something to laugh about. He was dressed in a loud Hawaiian-print shirt and shorts, even though it was THE MIDDLE OF WINTER! Dark sunglasses perched on his nose. A bracelet of green wooden beads dangled from his wrist. A tattoo on his right forepaw screamed **Aloha, Mousey**!

I was starting to feel ill. Oh, why did I think a friend of Trap's would be normal? This one looked like he belonged in a wild rat rock band!

I glanced around the room. It was packed with strange objects. They looked like

souvenirs from around the world. An
ENORMOUSE
stuffed cat's head hung on one
wall. I jumped. It looked
so real! I saw a bow and
a case filled with arrows.
A small card next to the
arrows warned:

CAREFUL, POISONOUS ARROWS!

I jumped again. Cheese niblets! This place
was dangerous. Other **CHEESY** souvenirs
filled the office. A large papier-mâché
Buddha mouse sat on the mantelpiece. A
collection of yellow rubber ducks from the
Quack Islands lined one wall.
A tacky sequined singing sombrero with
blinking red lights lay on a desk. This
place was like a flea market—a flea

market filled with nothing but junk!

Oh, why had I listened to my cousin? I should have gone to Kick Up Your Paws. At least *their* office is tastefully decorated. They even offer you a cheese snack when you walk in the door. Yes, that place was definitely more my style. Classy. Sophisticated. Safe.

Just then, an ear-piercing shriek filled the room. I **jumPed** so high, I nearly hit the ceiling. Trap snickered. "See, Smoothie," he said to the sleazy-looking rodent, "I told you

my cousin Geronimo is a scaredy mouse."

It was then that I noticed the plastic cuckoo clock. A sickly-looking bird had popped out of the clock door. It shrieked out the hour, then slid back inside.

Smoothie Slickpaws took off his sunglasses and shot me a sly smile. "WELL, HELLO, GERATTIMO!" he SHRIEKED, even louder than the cuckoo.

"YOUR NAME IS GERATTIMO, RIGHT?"

I shook my head. "Ahem, well no, actually, the name is *Geronimo*, Geronimo Stilton," I corrected him.

He waved me over to a chair. "Sit down, sit down, GERATTIMO," he squeaked. "Don't worry about a thing. I've got your vacation all planned out. Trust me, you'll like it!"

He winked at Trap. I wondered what that was all about. But there was no time to think about it. I had to get out of this place. I didn't want some TACKY mouse planning my precious vacation.

"First of all, my name is *Geronimo*, Geronimo Stilton. And I'm sorry, but I've changed my mind . . ." I began.

Trap didn't let me finish. "Remember, Smoothie, only the **best** will do for my cousin," he interrupted. He went on and on about how much money I had. Then he told Smoothie I needed to leave as soon as possible. "Just in case he changes his mind," Trap added, *winking* at his friend. "Maybe you could book him a flight for tomorrow. Or maybe even tonight."

At this point, my head was spinning. **Tomorrow? Tonight? "But what about my luggage?"** I protested. I am very big on packing. I like to be prepared. What if I forgot my fur brush? Or my underwear? Or my jumbo box of plastic bandages? Hey, you never know. I could cut my paw on a seashell or something.

SMOOTHIE rolled his eyes. "Who needs luggage, Gerattimo?" he laughed. "All you need on one of my vacations is yourself! **TRUST ME**, you'll like it!"

BUT I DON'T
WANT TO GO

I chewed my **whiskers**. What was wrong with this rodent? Were his ears filled with cheese? I opened my mouth to tell him my name was *Geronimo*, Geronimo Stilton, but it was no use. The tacky cuckoo clock had started **SHRIEKING** again (I guess it was broken). And Smoothie was already typing away like a madmouse at his computer. He spouted out names and times and dates.

"Let's see, departure at seven twenty-five from Mouse Island, arrival at ten fifty-six at San Shabby Fur Island, then there's the three-hour transfer..."

he babbled.

I tried to stop him, but he **IGNORED** me. His eyes were glued to the computer screen. He reminded me of my nephew Slowpoke when he's playing a video game. There's no tearing that mouse away from his games.

Meanwhile, Trap began reading aloud from a brochure. "Room with an *ocean* view... complimentary organic drink upon arrival... souvenir shop on the premises..." he rattled off. "This sounds

SAN SHABBY FUR ISLAND

incredible, Cousinkins. And it says here the 'personalized' transfer is included in the price!"

I was **in a daze**. I couldn't listen to both of them at the same time. Plus, my ears were still ringing from that **SINGING SOMBRERO**.

Smoothie asked me something, and I nodded. I could not hear one squeak.

At that moment, Smoothie **FLICKED OFF** his computer. He turned off the

SINGING SOMBRERO.

Then he shook my paw. "**OK, I did it!**" he announced. "I've booked you a place, Gerattimo. You're flying out in two hours!"

My stomach **LURCHED**. "Whaaat?" I stammered. "B-b-b-but I've decided I don't want to go."

Smoothie stroked his whiskers. "Sorry, Gerattimo, no can do. You nodded when I asked you if you wanted to book," he explained. "Now pack your bags. It's all settled."

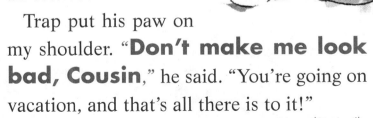

Trap put his paw on my shoulder. "**Don't make me look bad, Cousin**," he said. "You're going on vacation, and that's all there is to it!"

He turned to Smoothie and **winked**. Then they danced around the office.

HMMM. Something didn't seem quite right. Why was my cousin so interested in my vacation plans? I just couldn't put my paw on it. Oh, well.

TWO MINUTES LATER, I had my paw on something else. It was a bill for my upcoming vacation.

Smoothie snickered under his sleeve. Trap chuckled behind his whiskers.

I **stared** at the bill. A long string of numbers danced before my eyes.

INSTANTLY, I FAINTED.

Holey cheese!

MOVE YOUR TAIL!

When I came to, I held up the bill. "Isn't this price a little, um, **expensive**?" I stammered.

Trap shot me a look of pure pity, shaking his head. "Oh, Germeister, you are so behind the times. You really know nothing about the cost of things these days, do you?" he scoffed. "Tsk, tsk."

Before I could object, Smoothie jumped in.

"If you can't afford this vacation, you should have said so, Gerattimo," he added smugly. "Of course, I do offer rodents with financial troubles the option to pay in installments."

My fur turned bright **red**.

I was so *embarrassed.*

I didn't want Smoothie to think I was a cheapskate.

"Well, of course I can pay for this vacation," I *MUTTERED*. I pulled out my checkbook. "And if the place really is so beautiful and classy, naturally I can understand the expense."

Trap grabbed the check from my paw. "Naturally, naturally," he repeated, slapping me on the shoulder. "Now, move your tail, Cousinkins, or you'll miss your plane!"

"*Bon voyage!*" Smoothie shrieked. He pushed me out the door. I grabbed my tail before it got **squashed** like a pancake.

Thirty-five minutes later, I was at the airport. I was a **nervous wreck**. Did I mention I'm not into last-minute decisions? Still, I have to admit, I was a little excited.

My relaxing vacation was about to begin.

Before leaving, I called my sister, Thea. She's *The Rodent Gazette*'s special correspondent.

RINGGGGG RINGGGGG

She would take over the newspaper while I was away. Afterward, I called my favorite nephew, Benjamin. He is just a little mouselet, but he has the biggest heart I know. I love him more than all the cheese in the world.

"Have a great time, Uncle Geronimo!" he squeaked. "I can't wait to hear all about it when you get back."

LAST GASP AIRWAYS

At last, I climbed on board the plane. I was a little concerned. I had never flown LGA (Last Gasp Airways) before.

The first thing I noticed was the seats. They looked old and worn. The windows were streaked with dirt. And there were dust balls in the aisle.

I found my seat and sat down. It was hard as a rock. My tail was aching already. And what was that awful smell? I pulled a moldy cheese sandwich out from between the cushions. How FOUL.

I was wedged between an elderly lady and a young mouselet.

The elderly lady was very excited. She whispered she had never flown before.

"Don't worry," I told her. "Everything will be just fine." I'm **AFRAID** of flying, but I hoped she couldn't tell.

The young mouse on my other side made faces at me. Then he stole the cream cheese candy the flight attendant had just offered me.

"**Bratfur!** Give that candy back to the gentlemouse, now!" shouted his mother.

He smirked, then took the candy out of his mouth. "Want it back?" he slobbered.

I shook my snout in **DISGUST**. He scarfed it down. Then he stuck his tongue out at me.

I felt a headache coming on. *Relax,* I told myself. *You're on vacation. Don't let a little mouselet ruin your day.*

Seconds later, Bratfur began **PESTERING** me with questions.

"Why is San Shabby Fur Island called San

The young mouse stole my cream cheese candy.

Shabby Fur? Why does the plane have two engines instead of four? Why does the toilet make such a funny noise when I flush it? Why do you have fur sticking out of your nose?" he squeaked.

Meanwhile, Bratfur's mother shot me a proud smile. "MY LITTLE DARLING IS ALWAYS SO CURIOUS. I just know he's going to do great things someday!" she beamed.

I forced a smile. *Maybe I could take a nap,* I decided. But before I could even close my eyes, **BRATFUR** began chattering again. "Why can't I open the window? Why hasn't the flight attendant brought our lunch yet? Why are they showing that movie? Why do I have to keep my seat belt fastened? Why are you wearing those FUNNY glasses?" he babbled.

I grabbed my headphones. Maybe I could

listen to some music. Then Bratfur would bother someone else. Yes, that would do the trick. I put on my favorite station, *Calmmouse 101.9*. Ah, the soothing music filled my ears.

Something else filled my ears, too. RANCID RAT HAIRS! Bratfur was still talking to me. But now he was shrieking at the top of his lungs.

"Why can't I go to the toilet now? Why is the FASTEN YOUR SEAT BELTS sign on? Why is the mouse over there putting his finger in his NOSE? Why are there CLOUDS? Why are your ears so BIG?" he yelled.

By now, my head was about to explode. I couldn't take it anymore. I pictured myself tossing Bratfur out the emergency exit. I could just read the headline now: STILTON MURDERS MOUSELET! PUBLISHER PUSHED over the Edge by Nonstop Squeaking!

At that moment, I heard a seat belt click.

"Why can't I fly the **plane?** *"*

Bratfur shouted. He stormed into the pilot's cabin.

I watched in HORROR as he launched himself onto the control stick. *Cheese niblets!* Is this how it would all end? Killed in a plane crash by a chatterbox mouselet? I saw my life flash before my eyes.

"Why are you sleeping?" a squeaky voice shrieked in my ear.

My eyes flew open. Bratfur was back.

"I got him just in the nick of time," the flight attendant told his mom. My head began to **POUND** again. Maybe crashing wouldn't have been so bad after all.

THE FLYING TOMATO

The flight attendant began to serve lunch. I nibbled on a cracker. It tasted like cardboard.

Next I tried some **blue cheese soup**. It was SOUR.

I cut into the rubbery chicken. It slipped under my knife and landed in my suit pocket.

Sauce dribbled down my jacket. Oh, what a horrible flight! First Bratfur. Now the food.

My tummy grumbled in protest. CHEESE NIBLETS, I was hungry! I jabbed my fork into a small tomato on my plate. It SHOT away like a rocket, hitting the rodent across the aisle.

He glared at me. I gulped. He was one big mouse. I'm not talking just an extra-large. He was an **extra-mega-gigundo-large**. Lucky for me, right then they switched off the lights. The movie started. Everyone stared at the screen. It was a nail-biting *THRILLER*. I was glad I had already seen it. I don't like **SCARY MOVIES**. I have to watch them with all of the lights on. Plus, I like to hug my Cheesy the Rat doll at the really scary parts. But don't tell my family. They'd never stop picking on me if they knew I still had Cheesy.

I decided to take a nap. I was so exhausted.

I was half asleep when Bratfur began asking me questions about the movie. "Why is that mouse making so many cheddar cupcakes?" he whined. "Is he going to a birthday party? Is he a chef?"

"No, he's not a chef," I answered,

absentmindedly. "The cupcakes are filled with poison. He's **THE MURDERER**."

Bratfur let out a shriek. He jumped to his paws. "**Listen up, everybody!**" he yelled at the top of his lungs.

"**Those are poison cupcakes. That mouse is the murderer! The cheesebrain sitting beside me just told me!**"

All of the passengers gave me nasty looks.

I cringed. Those poison cupcakes were starting to look pretty good.

Suddenly, *the plane began to shake.*

"All rodents kindly fasten your seat belts!" announced the captain.

The elderly lady next to me looked worried.

"There's nothing to worry about, madam," I assured her. "It's just a little turbulence. It will all be over soon."

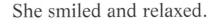

The 8 Stages of Airsickness:

1. Distracted look

2. Deathly pallor, cold sweats

She smiled and relaxed.

But ten minutes later, the plane was still rocking. I began to turn **green**. ONE MINUTE WE WERE UP, THE NEXT WE WERE DOWN. Did I mention I have a weak stomach?

Meanwhile, the elderly lady next to me didn't seem to notice. She began chatting away. "I can't wait to get to San Shabby Fur Island. I hear they have the best octopus-and-garlic soup," she squeaked

3. Stomach cramps

4. Rolling eyes, olive-green complexion

happily. "Then again, I think they're known for their *oily sardine pizzas*."

By now, my stomach was gurgling up a storm. I felt so sick, I could hardly breathe. *Please don't mention food again*, I wanted to squeak. But the old lady kept rattling on and on. Oh, why was she so OBSESSED with food? Didn't they feed her down at the Creaky Mouse Nursing Home?

8. Cheese niblets!

7. Monstrous burps

5. Lizard-green complexion

6. Pistachio-green complexion

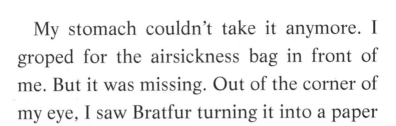
My stomach couldn't take it anymore. I groped for the airsickness bag in front of me. But it was missing. Out of the corner of my eye, I saw Bratfur turning it into a paper airplane.

I wanted to **STRANGLE** him, but I didn't have any strength left.

"Who can lend me a bag? A bag! I'm going to throw up!" I shrieked at the top of my voice.

Everyone stared at me in shock. How embarrassing. The flight attendant came running. But unfortunately, it was too late.

When we reached San Shabby Fur, everyone dashed off the plane. I could tell they wanted to get away from me. I did, too. I was a stinky mess!

Bratfur turned the bag into a paper airplane.

SAN SHABBY
FUR ISLAND

I headed for baggage claim.

On the way there...

AN ENORMOUSE BAGGAGE HANDLER

...with bulging muscles ran over my tail with his cart...

...a lady mouse stomped on my paw with her **high heels**...

He-he-heee...

...Bratfur threw a glass of **orange juice** all over my best suit jacket...

...I lost the keys to my suitcase...

...I stopped in the restroom and dropped my passport into the toilet bowl.

It took me a while to fish out my passport. By then, I was ready to **cry**. So I sat down on the luggage carousel and began to sob like my cousin Wimpy Whiskers the time he got hit on the head with a Wiffle ball. Right then, the carousel began to move. **Slimy Swiss rolls**! My tail

HELPP!!!

was stuck in the **gears**. I yanked it out.

After **TWENTY** minutes, I spotted my suitcase. Then I saw it again and again. Yep, there were seven suitcases that looked just like mine! I had to **wrestle** my bag away from a lady mouse who insisted it was hers.

At last, I was ready to leave the airport. I held out my passport to the customs mouse.

IT'S MY SUITCASE!

It was *stinky*, just like me.

I left the airport exhausted. It was already late at night. I was dying to reach my hotel.

Outside it was pouring rain. I looked around for the mouse who was supposed to meet me from the TRUST ME, YOU'LL LIKE IT! travel agency.

I spotted a slimy-looking rat carrying a sign:

> WELCOME,
> GERATTIMO STILTON.
> TRUST ME, YOU'LL LIKE IT!

WELCOME,
GERATTIMO
STILTON.
TRUST ME,
YOU'LL LIKE IT!

I waved him over. "Are you GERATTIMO STILTON?" he asked, looking me over.

I shook my head. "Yes, I mean, no, I mean the name is Geronimo. Geronimo Stilton."

He stared down at his sign. "But it says here 'Gerattimo,'" he squeaked.

I took a deep breath. I practiced a little meditation exercise I had learned. "Remain calm," I chanted under my breath. "Don't get upset."

"They must have gotten it wrong at the agency," I explained in a slow voice. "My name is Geronimo. G-E-R-O-N-I-M-O," I repeated.

The mouse scratched his whiskers. "Are you **sure**?"

By now I was ready to **EXPLODE**. So much for that meditation class I took last year. Maybe I could get my money back. *"Moldy mozzarella balls! Of course I'm sure!"* I screeched. *"Don't you think I know my own name?"*

He shrugged his shoulders. "If you say so..." he muttered.

Meanwhile rain had **SOAKED** through my fur. "Does it always rain so hard here?" I asked.

The rat from the Trust Me, You'll Like It travel agency blinked. "Didn't they tell you?" he snickered. "On the island, it either pours or it's *SO HOT* you can fry your own fur."

I put my head in my paws. I knew I shouldn't have trusted my cousin and that slick rat Smoothie.

WHAT WHAT WHAT?

The next thing I knew, the rat had brought me to a back parking lot. He pointed to a beat-up old bicycle with a funny-looking cart attached to it.

"*Here you are!*" he announced.

I stared at the strange contraption. "Wh-wh-what do you m-m-mean?" I stammered.

He pulled a piece of paper out of his pocket. It said: ———▶

"You see, this is your personalized transfer," he explained. "You need to pedal in person. The **RATHOLE HOTEL** is only twenty miles away."

PASSENGER NOTE: GERATTIMO STILTON PERSONALIZED TRANSFER.

My head began to pound. Steam shot out my ears. I am usually a very reserved rodent, but this was just too much. It was time to put my paw down.

"**WHAT?**" I shrieked so loud, I made myself jump. *"Are you saying I've got to ride that bike for twenty miles? At night? Alone? In the pouring rain? Carrying my own luggage?"* I was growing madder by the minute. *"Well, there's no way that's going to happen, you mad mousey!"* I cried. *"Absolutely no possible way! No ifs, ands, or buts! No can do! Not on your life!* **Not for all the cheddar roll-ups in the world! I totally and completely refuse, or my name is not** *Geronimo Stilton!"*

TRULY A RAT'S NEST

Ten minutes later, I was **PEDALING AWAY** into the night. I really needed to talk to my therapist about becoming **MORE ASSERTIVE**.

The rain pounded down on my head. I choked back tears. My best suit was getting ruined. How would I explain this one to Starchette? Do you know her? She's the cute mouse who works down at my dry cleaners'.

I started off on the main road but soon found myself on a dirt path. It led into a deep, dark forest. Rat-munching rattlesnakes! Things were going from **bad to worse!**

The sky grew darker and darker. I tried to light the way with the tiny flashlight

attached to my key ring. It didn't work. I felt like my cousin Squinty before he got glasses. Everything was pitch-black.

Suddenly, the bicycle's front wheel hit a stone. The cart turned over. My suitcase flew into the air and landed on my tail. "Cheese niblets!" I squeaked. *"I KNEW I SHOULDN'T HAVE TRUSTED THEM!"*

Right then, I heard the **S🅞UND 🅞F FARAWAY MUSIC.** It gave me hope. Guided by the music, I pedaled for another fifteen minutes. Then I reached a clearing in the forest.

I noticed a weathered old sign. It read:

RATHOLE HOTEL

"Safe at last!" I murmured happily. But my happiness didn't last long.

I pulled up to the hotel. It was a

THREE-STORY WOODEN SHACK

with a collapsed roof and broken windows. At the entrance lay a doormat full of holes. From the doorknob hung an **ELCOME** sign.

The "**W**" was missing.

I stumbled off the bike. I was dizzy from all the exercise. Spots swam before my eyes. Still, one thing was clear to me. The **RATHOLE HOTEL** was definitely *a rat hole!*

The Rathole Hotel was definitely a rat hole!

ROOM 313!

I parked the bike in front of the entrance. Then I dragged my suitcase up to the door. **Why, oh, why** had I brought so much stuff? I crawled toward the reception desk, grumbling and groaning.

There was no one in sight. I put my paw on the bell and began to ring. I rang and rang and rang **FURIOUSLY** for at least ten minutes.

Finally, a plump mouse with thick handlebar whiskers held in place with clothespins sauntered out.

He was wearing a brightly striped T-shirt and loud Bermuda shorts. He yawned into my snout and mumbled, "Well?"

"Yes, I have a reservation here," I squeaked. "My name is Stilton, Geronimo Stilton."

He scratched his tail.

"Ummm, let's see…here it says you are *Gerattimo* Stilton," he muttered. "Are you sure your name is Geronimo?"

I gnashed my teeth. My whiskers began to whirl in a rage. Why would no one listen to me? Did they *all* have cheese in their ears?

"Of course I'm sure! I ought to know my own name," I exploded.

"So please take note that my name is Geronimo, Geronimo Stilton!

And that I'm fed up! That I'm exhausted!

That I want to go to my room now! That I want to take a shower!

That I want to eat something! And most of all that I want to be called Geronimo!

Ge-ro-ni-mo! G-e-r-o-n-i-m-o!!!

He shot me a look of pity. "Whatever," he said with a yawn. "Guess it's a good thing you decided to take a vacation. You sure are one stressed-out rodent."

He grabbed a key and slapped it into my paw. "You're on the third floor," he told me. "And don't look for the elevator. We don't have one. By the way, the restaurant is closed. But as our brochure says, you'll find *a delicious welcoming snack* on your bedside table."

ONE SMELLY CHEESE RIND

I climbed the WOODEN staircase, lugging my suitcase behind me.

It was then that I realized I would be staying in room **313**.

Three hundred *thirteen*! HOLEY CHEESE!

Are you superstitious? I'M NOT REALLY.

Well, MAYBE A LITTLE. OK, MAYBE A LOT. My teeth began to chatter just thinking about the number thirteen. How unlucky can you get?!

I reached my door and opened it. I switched on the light...

...and almost fainted.

I tried to remember the description of the room in the brochure.

How unlucky can you get?!

...uniquely decorated...
...sea view...
...bathtub with organic hydromassage...
...own fridge...
...own television...

I looked around. No fridge. No television. Instead, I found a **dark, dingy** room painted a sickly green. The one window overlooked an open-air disco. Below, hundreds of rodents were dancing wildly to the rhythm of **EAR-PIERCING** music.

I stumbled to the bathroom, clutching my nose. Did I mention the place smelled? Instead of a bathtub there was a **large, rusty metal bucket**.

This is not happening, I told myself. *This is all just a bad dream.*

I sat down on the **WORM-EATEN** bed and closed my eyes. Inhale...exhale, I chanted. Yes, I was starting to feel a teeny-tiny bit better. Two minutes later, I heard a loud crack. Then the bed collapsed under my weight!

I opened my eyes. That's when I spotted the plate on my bedside table. It held a piece of **STALE** bread and one smelly **cheese rind**. A plastic fork with a

BROKEN tine was stuck in the rind.

The plate had been *decorated* with a big lettuce leaf. A snail sat in the middle of the leaf, munching away. There was an olive pit next to the leaf. I guess the snail liked olives, too.

I chewed my whiskers in frustration.

Was this the "delicious snack"? Was this the "welcome"? Was this a joke?

At that moment, I noticed a small greasy card by the plate. I read it out loud:

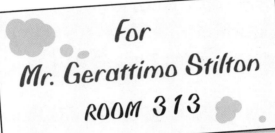

**For
Mr. Gerattimo Stilton
ROOM 313**

"**Gerattimo?!**" I squeaked, feeling the blood rush to my fur. "**GERATTIMO? GERATTIMO?**" I repeated, paws clenched. "**CHEESE NIBLETS!**"

I threw the window open and stuck my head out. "My name is Geronimo, Geronimo Stilton!!!"

I screeched.

The loud music from the disco stopped

abruptly. A hundred rodents turned to face my window.

"Who's that MADMOUSE?" I heard one mouse whisper.

"Must be some kinda WACKO," another squeaked.

"TOO MUCH SUN, if you ask me," a third voice added.

Ashamed, I closed the window and drew the curtains.

What I need is a nice hot shower, I decided.

I lathered myself with SOAP and turned on the tap. Not a single drop of water came out! I stumbled to the phone to call the lobby. I should have known. The line was dead.

I stamped my paw in **DISGUST** and slipped on the dirty carpet. "I knew I shouldn't have trusted them," I groaned.

I was too TiRed to go downstairs to complain. I was too tired to unpack my suitcase. I was too tired to cry.

No, there was only one thing left to do. I pulled on a pair of dirty white pajamas I found hanging in the bathroom. Then I threw myself down on the smelly bed to try and get some sleep.

COCKROACHES
FOR BREAKFAST

The next morning, I woke up exhausted, with bags under my eyes. 👁

CHEESE NIBLETS! What a night! I was kept awake by a swarm of fleas in my bed. And the noisy disco hadn't shut down until five in the morning.

I would have loved to sleep late, but I couldn't. At six o'clock, I practically flew out of my bed. A construction crew had begun DRILLING and HAMMERING right under my window. The noise was even worse than the disco music.

I headed toward the bathroom without my glasses. I was too tired to put them on.

I switched on the light, yawning.

HOW STRANGE. I COULD HAVE SWORN THE BATHROOM TILES WERE ALL WHITE, NOT BLACK, I mumbled to myself.

Right then, I lay my paw on one of the small black tiles. A terrible **CRUNCHING** noise followed.

My stomach lurched. Something told me this wasn't a **GOOD SIGN**.

 **I RAN** for my glasses. Did I tell you I can't see a thing without them?

Back in the bathroom, I discovered a

horrifying sight. I had **squashed** a **COCKROACH!** The bathroom was full of them. Giant cockroaches everywhere, on the floor, on the walls, and even on the ceiling.

At that very moment, a cockroach fell off the ceiling and landed inside the collar of my pajamas. It crawled all the way down my back.

I let out a **HORRIFIED SCREAM** that woke the entire hotel.

Ten seconds later, someone banged on the wall.

"What's going on?" I heard a mouse ask.

"Who screamed?" another cried.

"It's that Stilton again,

Gerattimo Stilton," someone else answered. I cringed behind the door. How embarrassing. I listened to the crowd gathering in the hallway. They were all talking. Yes, talking about yours truly.

"**Him again?**" a rodent huffed.

"Yes, it's that **cheesebrain** who arrived yesterday," a voice grumbled.

"Ah, you mean the mouse who wants to be **THE CENTER OF ATTENTION?**" a rodent muttered.

"**TOO MUCH SUN**, if you ask me," someone else muttered.

I had stopped screaming. But now I was purple with shame!

I Can't Open My Suitcase!!!

I went to look for my toothbrush. Then I remembered I had lost the key to my suitcase. I tried all the ways I could think of to open the lock. First I inserted a paper clip. Then I tried picking it with a cheese knife. I even tried **HAMMERING** the lock with the doorstop. Still, it wouldn't budge.

Getting more desperate by the minute, I smashed it against the wall.

NOTHING HAPPENED.

I was ready to smash myself against the wall. I needed my stuff! I wanted to brush my teeth. I wanted to put on a clean pair of underwear.

"Rats!" I shrieked, giving the suitcase a hard kick. It went flying out **OVER THE BALCONY.**

I scrambled downstairs to go get it. It still hadn't opened.

I dragged it back to my room. Then I sat down on it and c r i e d .

What else could I do?

I'M TOO SEXY FOR MY FUR!

I decided the first thing to do was buy myself a new swimsuit.

I went in search of the hotel's *gift shop.*

The store was dark and dusty. A scruffy-looking mouse sat with his paws up on the counter.

"**I need a bathing suit**," I told him.

He pointed to a rack. There was only one swimsuit hanging from it. It had **purple-and-yellow stripes** with two tacky satin hearts. The tag inside read I'M TOO SEXY FOR MY FUR!

It was the most hideous thing I have ever seen. Plus, it was **three sizes too big** for me.

"Do you have something less flashy in a

smaller size?" I asked the salesclerk.

He shook his head. "Nope, that's it. Take it or leave it."

I blinked. "But this one doesn't fit me," I protested. "And besides, I don't like it."

"Well, then don't take it," he mumbled.

"But I need it!" I cried.

"WELL, THEN TAKE IT!" he shouted in my ear.

I pulled out my wallet to pay for the swimsuit. That's when I saw the price tag.

DOLLAR SIGNS swam before my eyes. "Why is this so expensive?!" I shrieked.

"**It's ONE of a kind**," the sales clerk smirked. "You'll make a real fashion statement."

I groaned. I'd make a real statement, all right. I'd be the most ridiculous-looking rodent on the beach!

Everything A.P.B. (As Per Brochure)

I went to speak with the hotel manager. My whiskers were quivering in anger. I had a list of complaints a mile long. I mean, the brochure listed this place as a resort. But it was clearly a dump.

The manager listened to me with a funny look on his face. He didn't seem too surprised by my gripes. "Come with me and I'll explain everything," he said.

We went up to my room. Then he began to read from the brochure. "Let's see, you booked *a room with unique decorating features*," he read. He waved his paw around the room. "Have you ever seen a room painted in such a shade of moldy green? Pretty *unique*, wouldn't you say?" He grinned. "Therefore, **it is A.P.B. (AS PER BROCHURE).**"

My head began to pound. "But what about the *sea view?*" I protested.

He snickered. I was getting the impression I wasn't the first rodent to complain.

He pulled out a small pair of binoculars from his pocket. "OK, if you lean out as far as you can over the balcony, turn left, stretch your neck, pop out your eyes, and use these binoculars, you'll have your sea view! Yep, **tHat's A.P.B. (AS PER BROCHURE).**"

I chewed my whiskers. "B-b-but what about the *b-b-bathtub with the organic hydromassage?*"

Once again he snickered. He went into the bathroom and pointed to the dented washtub.

"Here is your *tub*," he said. Then he pulled an eggbeater from his other pocket. "And here is your *hydromassage!*"

He put the beater into the water and began **TURNING IT FURIOUSLY**.

"See what I mean? Yep, **THaT'S A.P.B (AS PeR BRoCHURe)** for sure!" he chuckled.

By now, I was seething with rage. "But what about having my *own fridge* and my *own television?*"

"Well, that's pretty obvious!" the manager chuckled. "It means you should have brought your *own!* Yessiree, that one is **Definitely A.P.B. (AS PER BROCHURE)!**"

Finally, I couldn't take it anymore. I was so mad, I had twisted my tail up like a pretzel.

"**BROCHURE?!**" I exploded. "I don't give a whisker about the brochure! This place is ridiculous! This place is preposterous! This place isn't fit for a flea!"

Just then, someone from next door banged on the wall. I could hear the comments flying:

"Who's the MADMOUSE shouting at the top of his lungs?" someone cried.

"It's that **Stilton** again, **Gerattimo Stilton**," another squeaked.

"He's really **lost his marbles now!**" a third rodent added.

"TOO MUCH SUN, if you ask me," someone else muttered.

How embarrassing.

A RUBBERY
BREAD ROLL

I decided a nice breakfast would cheer me up. There was **A LONG LINE** of mice leading into the dining room.

"Did you get your number?" a mouse with a terribly burned snout asked me.

"Number? What number?" I asked.

Snout Burn pointed to the line. "The number for your place in line. It takes at least **three hours** to get breakfast around here," he said.

I sighed. I knew I shouldn't have trusted them!

I took my place in line. My stomach was grumbling like my uncle Cheesebelly when they run out of cheese rolls at the bakery. I hadn't eaten anything since that awful cheese rind the night before. I was starving. Just then, I noticed a mouse carrying a tray of bread rolls, tea, and coffee for sale. I couldn't resist. I was so hungry. I bought a small roll and a cup of coffee. The roll tasted like **rubber**. The coffee tasted like mud.

"That'll be thirty bucks, please," squeaked the mouse.

"What?" I squeaked. "THAT'S HIGHWAY ROBBERY!"

The mouse just snickered. "Take it or leave it."

What could I do? I paid him the money.

Rats! I knew I shouldn't have trusted them!

HOW MUCH FARTHER TO THE BEACH???

After breakfast, I headed for the beach. I followed the long path through the sand dunes. I walked and walked and walked. An hour later, I was still walking. Did I mention the path was long? The SUN SCORCHED my fur. I was dying of thirst. I mean, really DYING.

Suddenly, I had a horrifying thought. What if I really *did* die of thirst? Headlines flashed before my eyes: STILTON SIZZLES TO A CRISP! PARCHED PUBLISHER: ALL DRIED UP AND NO PLACE TO GO!

Just then, I spotted something up ahead. It was a lemonade stand. "How much farther

to the beach?" I asked the vendor.

He smirked. "Just another hour," he said.

I felt faint. Another hour? I would never make it!

I gulped down a glass of LEMONADE.

"That'll be fifty $MACKEROO$. Cash only," the mouse said, grinning evilly.

I pulled out my wallet. What else could I do?

I knew I shouldn't have **TRUSTED** them!

A Scooter Worth Its Weight in Gold

I kept on walking under the burning sun. After a little while, I saw another vendor. This one was renting out scooters.

"Ahem, how much for a scooter?" I asked cautiously.

"Don't worry, we take credit cards," the mouse replied.

I IMMEDIATELY STARTED WORRYING.

This little vacation was costing me a fortune! I was going to have to eat only **mac and cheese** when I got back home. Yep, no more fancy dinners for me after this trip. I was going **BROKE**!

Just as I thought, the scooter was worth its weight in gold. At last, I reached the beach. I looked like a TRAIN WRECK. My tongue was hanging out of my mouth from the heat. My snout was *SUNBURNED*. And my left paw was longer than my right paw. Oh, but that's another story.

I was welcomed by a lifeguard as **big** as a house. He was wearing an itty-bitty yellow bathing suit and an extra-tight tank top that read **Rathole Hotel Beach**. On his bulging right bicep, he had a tattoo of a *beautiful female mouse.* He had a THICK GOLD CHAIN around his neck, and his hair GLEAMED in the sun. What an athlete! What a muscle mouse! *What a show-off!*

He held out his paw. "Call me **CRUSHER**,"

Rathole Hotel Beach

CRUSHER

he said, squeezing my paw in his. I yelped. When he released me, I checked for BROKEN BONES.

Crusher didn't seem to notice my pain. He pulled out a pad with a list of names on it.

"You must be GERATTIMO STILTON," he said. "I've been expecting you."

"*Geronimo*, not *Gerattimo*," I corrected him wearily.

He stared at the pad again. "Are you sure your name is *Geronimo?*" he mumbled. "It says *Gerattimo* here."

I was so tired I could barely squeak. "My name is *Geronimo, Geronimo Stilton,*" I whispered.

He scratched his tail. "If you say so..." he **muttered**. I could tell he didn't believe me.

SUCH A PLAYFUL MOUSE...

Crusher led me to my beach umbrella. The tag said:

313 - GeRATTiMO STiLTON!

I pretended not to see it so I wouldn't have to complain. Instead, I looked around. The beach was mobbed. The rat sitting on my left had his radio cranked up to an **earsplitting** volume. On my right sat Bratfur. Yes, it was that obnoxious young mouselet who had been sitting next to me on the plane. Rats! I had the worst luck!

As he was leaving, Crusher pointed to the water. Then he shouted something, but I couldn't hear him. The music was so **loud**.

The beach was mobbed.

"What did you say?" I shouted.

But he was already **gone**.

Two minutes later, I got hit with a bucketful of ice-cold water.

I whipped around. Then I sighed. It was Bratfur, of course.

His mother smiled. "He's such a nice playful mouse, don't you think?" she laughed.

I shut my snout. I was following my aunt Sweetfur's advice. She always told me, "If you don't have anything nice to squeak, don't squeak anything at all."

As Pale as a Piece of Mozzarella

It didn't take Bratfur long to begin pestering me with his questions. "Why is the sun *HOT*? Why is the water *WET*? Why does the sand *BURN* your paws? Why does the lifeguard have all those muscles? Why don't you have any muscles?" he chattered.

I pretended to be asleep. It didn't stop him. "Why do I have to put on *SUNTAN LOTION*? Why was it raining yesterday and today it's sunny? Why do fish like water? Why do seagulls have white poop? Why are you as pale as a piece of mozzarella?" he babbled.

Meanwhile, the rat on my left was tapping his paw to the rhythm of the music. He was kicking up clouds of sand.

"Er, excuse me, could you stop covering me in sand?" I asked him politely.

"What BAND? There's no band here!" he replied.

I shook my head. "No, the sand!" I repeated a little louder this time.

He looked confused. "What? Land? No, planes don't **LAND** here!" he yelled.

I chewed my whiskers. "Not land. I said SAND!" I shrieked.

The rat just shrugged his shoulders. He closed his eyes and started tapping his paw even faster to the beat of the music.

Finally, I couldn't take it anymore. I switched off his radio and shouted at the top of my lungs, "Sand! SAAND! You're

covering me in

SAAAAAAAAAND!"

The beach grew silent. I looked around. Everyone was staring at me.

"It's him again, isn't it?" I heard one bather comment.

"Yes, it's that Gerattimo Stilton!" another replied.

"What is his **problem?**" someone else asked.

"He should be ashamed of himself!" a rodent added.

"T☉☉ MUCH SUN, if you ask me..." another mumbled.

Purple with shame, I tried to hide behind my newspaper.

After a while I realized I *was* getting sunburned.

I decided to buy some suntan lotion. Right at that moment, I saw a peddler passing by. He pulled out a tiny tube of sunblock. "You'll need one with a **90** SPF. You're as pale as a piece of mozzarella!" he said knowingly. "That'll be **ONE HUNDRED BUCKAROO$**, please."

My eyes nearly popped out of my head. "What a rip-off!" I squeaked. Then I paid him.

Forget the cheese!

I WOULD ONLY BE ABLE TO AFFORD THE MACARONI AFTER THIS VACATION!!

SWIMMING WITH SHARKS

I decided to go for a swim. I noticed there wasn't a single mouse in the water. **Perfect!**

I put on my flippers, my bathing cap, and my earplugs and plunged in. I floated lazily out to the open sea. After a while, I noticed that a small boat was following me. The lifeguard on board waved his paws at me. It was Crusher. I guess he thought I might be afraid of the deep water. I waved back and smiled to let him know I was OK.

But Crusher kept following me. Then he started yelling something.

I took out my earplugs as the boat came closer.

"LOOK OUT FOR SHARKS!" I heard Crusher shriek. At the same time, I heard something else. A loud splashing sound right behind me. **Cheese niblets!** Out of the corner of my eye, I noticed a gleaming fin. A SHARK was right on my tail!

TEN SECONDS later, a paw reached out and grabbed me. It was Crusher. He pulled me onto his boat. Then he motored back to shore. "I told you to watch out for the sharks, Gerattimo," Crusher scolded me.

When I got out of the boat, everyone was staring at me.

The comments were flying.

"It's that Gerattimo Stilton again!" one rodent huffed.

"Swimming with the sharks just to get himself noticed!" another griped.

"What a **cheesehead**!" someone else snorted.

"**TOO MUCH SUN**, if you ask me..." another mouse mumbled.

How embarrassing! **QUIET AS A MOUSE**, I ducked under the umbrellas. Then I scampered away.

5:30 A.M.
BUNGEE JUMPING

It had been a **DISASTROUS** day.

I fell into bed, exhausted, that night.

Tomorrow I'm going to sleep until noon, I decided. I'm supposed to be on vacation, right? Or maybe I'd just stay in bed the whole day.

I fell into a restless sleep. The disco music

roared in my ears.

At five o'clock in the morning, I was woken up by a knock at my door.

"Who is it?" I mumbled.

"Wake up, Gerattimo! Time to leave!" squeaked a voice on the other side of the door.

I opened it. It was another muscle mouse. This one was even bigger than Crusher. He looked like he lifted weights in his sleep.

"Did you forget, Gerattimo?" he cried. "You're booked for a bungee-jumping lesson this morning."

I didn't understand. "WHAT? But I didn't..." I stammered.

Before I could go on, **MUSCLE MOUSE** stuck a piece of paper under my snout. It read:

> 5:30 A.M.: BUNGEE JUMPING—GERATTIMO STILTON
> 7:30 A.M.: HANG-GLIDING—GERATTIMO STILTON
> 11:30 A.M.: DEEP-SEA DIVING—GERATTIMO STILTON
> 12:30 P.M.: ARCHERY—GERATTIMO STILTON
> 2:00 P.M.: FREE-FALL PARACHUTING—GERATTIMO
>   STILTON
> 4:00 P.M.: DEEP-SEA FISHING (WITH SHARKS)—
>   GERATTIMO STILTON
> 7:00 P.M.: ROCK CLIMBING—GERATTIMO STILTON

MUSCLE MOUSE gave me a friendly slap on the back. It sent me flying across the room. I crashed into the dresser. I wondered if I was totally paralyzed or if I would be able to walk with a cane.

MUSCLE MOUSE didn't seem to notice my pain. "Are you telling me you've forgotten, Gerattimo?" he grinned.

I didn't know what to say. Of course, I hadn't signed up for such ridiculously dangerous activities. After all, I'm afraid of heights. I'm afraid of sharks. I'm afraid of pairing the wrong shirt with the wrong tie.

"Ahem, first of all, my name is *Geronimo, Geronimo* Stilton..." I corrected him.

He smirked, waving the piece of paper under my nose.

"**What a joker!**" he chuckled. "**It says here, 'Gerattimo.' And, Gerattimo, we've already wasted too much time. Now, get dressed and let's get going!**"

I tried to protest, but he kept waving the paper under my snout. But there was no way I was going. No way in a million, trillion, gazillion years!

Two minutes later, I followed **MUSCLE MOUSE** down the hall. I had fallen for the old "**shake my paw**" trick. When I stuck out my paw to shake, **MUSCLE MOUSE** had grabbed me.

Cheese niblets, it was going to be one long day!

WHISKERS QUIVERING . . .

What can I say?
The whole day
was an absolute
NIGHTMARE.
I jumped (or was I
pushed?) off a bridge with a rubber
band attached to my ankle . . .
Then I jumped (or was I pushed?)
off a cliff with a hang glider strapped
around me . . .
Next I plunged (or was I
pushed?) into the sea with
a **heavy** tank on my
back . . .
Yes, I think it would

be safe to say it was the worst day of my life. After the scuba diving, I went parachuting. I was so scared, I fainted on the way down. Then I swam with the SHARKS. I swam away so fast, I didn't stop until I hit my beach umbrella. Finally, I went rock climbing up Mount Deadrat. Frankly, I'm amazed I'm still alive and squeaking!

I headed back to the hotel with a **POUNDING** headache. What a frightening day. My whiskers were quivering with stress.

I dragged myself past the reception desk. That's when I noticed Bratfur. He was busy scribbling something on the EXTREME SPORTS ACTIVITIES BOARD.

I snuck up behind him. Rotten rats' teeth! He was writing my name down after every activity.

Enough was enough, I decided. It was time to give Bratfur a piece of my mind. But before I could squeak a word, his mother arrived. She gently took the pen from her son's paw. Then she stroked his ears. "My *little darling is such a silly joker,"* she murmured, leading him away. Bratfur stuck his tongue out at me.

Silly joker?! I wanted to scream. But I didn't. Instead, I thought about some "silly jokes" I could play on Bratfur. Like maybe I could put itching powder on his beach towel. Or I could stick chewing gum on his pillow. Or, even better, I could lock him in his suitcase and ship him off to Tomcat Island. I snickered just thinking about it. Yes, a few days with some tough cats would be just perfect for the

little darling!

Sea Lion Sweat Smoothie

It was dinnertime. I got in the long line.

Just then, a polished-looking female mouse strolled up to me. She offered me a glass of some strange-looking liquid.

"Hello, I'm Perky, your Health and Relaxation Director," she announced.

"You look like you could really use our services."

Perky chattered on about mud baths, steam saunas, and meditation classes. I was only half listening. Instead I was staring at the drink in my paw. It had the MOST DISGUSTING SMELL.

"What is this?" I asked, feeling ill.

"A sea lion sweat smoothie," she

answered. "It's loaded with vitamins and minerals."

I tried not to gag. As soon as Perky left, I started to empty the drink into a flowerpot.

Suddenly, she reappeared at my side. "You need to drink that," she squeaked. "It's good for you!"

I blinked. "Um, thank you, it's just that…"

"I said, drink it up. NOW!" she hissed.

I'd had enough. I put my paws on my hips. "I'M NOT GOING TO DRINK IT! IT STINKS!" I shrieked at the top of my lungs.

The room fell silent.

Everyone turned around.

"Who's yelling his head off?" I heard a mouse ask.

"Must be that Gerattimo Stilton again," another answered.

"TOO MUCH SUN, if you ask me," mumbled another rodent.

THERE MUST BE SOME MISTAKE!

That night, I fell into bed. *Tomorrow I will definitely sleep in*, I told myself.

But at six o'clock the next morning, someone was knocking at my door. "WHO IS IT NOW?" I asked, exasperated.

"It's the hotel manager, Gerattimo!" a voice squeaked. "Have you forgotten you are leaving today? You're very late! You're going to miss your plane!"

I opened the door **in a daze**. "What do you mean I'm leaving? I've paid for a whole week," I muttered.

The hotel manager just shook his head. He showed me a piece of paper from the **TRUST ME, YOU'LL LIKE IT!** travel agency. It read:

I was speechless.

> Gerattimo Stilton: booking for two nights

The hotel manager put his paw on my shoulder. "I know you want to stay longer, Gerattimo. The Rathole is such a *wonderful* hotel," he murmured. "But you must go home now. Better shake a paw. Remember, it's twenty miles to the airport. And if you don't leave now, the next available plane doesn't leave for another month."

THAT DID IT. There was no way I was spending another month on San Shabby Fur Island. I grabbed my suitcase. Then I jumped on the strange bicycle and took off like a madmouse.

It was a **VERY, VERY, VERY LONG** ride. Still, I managed to catch my plane just before it took off.

I collapsed into my seat and fell into a

DEEP, DEEP SLEEP.

The next thing I knew, a flight attendant was shouting in my ear. "Wake up, we've reached our destination, Mr. Gerattimo!"

Ah, sweet, sweet Mouse Island. I had never been so glad to be home. I smiled at the flight attendant. "The name's *Geronimo, Geronimo* Stilton…" I said with a yawn.

Outside the airport, I hailed a taxi. "**Take me to the** TRUST ME, YOU'LL LIKE IT! **travel agency, please**," I told the driver.

The taxi stopped in front of the agency.

I leaped out. But I didn't get far.

A card was stuck in the shop window.

CLOSED FOR VACATION.
—SMOOTHIE SLICKMOUSE
P.S. IN CASE OF AN EMERGENCY, PLEASE
CONTACT MY PARTNER, MR. TRAP STILTON

Just then, it hit me. Trap was Smoothie's partner. That's why he wanted me to book a trip with Smoothie. He was making money off me. Oh, what a cheesebrain I'd been!

I ran to my cousin's thrift shop, Cheap Junk for Less.

There was a card in this window, too.

CLOSED, SUPER-CLOSED, I'M AWAY, GOT IT? I'M AT THE HIGH-CLASS RODENT LUXURY RESORT. (NOT IN A RAT'S NEST LIKE THE ONE THAT MY **CHEESEBRAIN** COUSIN GERONIMO WENT TO.)

LAUGHTER IS CONTAGIOUS

I trudged to my office. I had to tell someone about my disastrous vacation. I poured out the whole story to my sister, Thea.

"Did you really swim with sharks? Did you really go bungee jumping? Did you really bike twenty miles to the hotel?" she snickered. Then she burst out laughing.

I was a bit hurt by her reaction. I had been looking for a shoulder to cry on. But Thea's shoulders were **shaking with laughter**. Tears streamed down her fur. "I haven't laughed this hard in years!" she shrieked. "Tell me again about the flashy bathing suit you bought. And were you really pestered by a mouselet named **BRATFUR**?"

Now, as every rodent knows, laughter is contagious. Before I knew it, I was chuckling, too.

I mean, when I really thought about it, my adventures were pretty funny.

The rest of my staff came in to see what all the noise was about. Soon my secretary, Mousella MacMouser; my editor in chief, Kreamy O'Cheddar; my art director, *Merenguita Gingermouse*; and my designers, Blasco Tabasco, Larry Keys, and Matt Wolf, were howling away with us. Even the cleaning mouse and the Xpress Delivery mouse joined in. Our laughter could be heard outside on the ███████. It infected many

My sales manager, Shif T. Paws, entered the room.

curious passersby. Everyone wanted to hear the details of my incredibly **AWFUL**, **UNBELIEVABLE**, ROTTEN, STINKING **NIGHTMARE** vacation.

Right then, my sales manager, Shif T. Paws, entered the room. Do you know him? He's a rodent with a nose for business. One look at the hysterical crowd and I could see Shif's eyes light up.

He immediately pulled me aside. "Stilton, start writing a book about your adventure **RIGHT AWAY!**" he ordered. "We're going to sell

thousands, no **millions**, no **billions** of copies.

Cheesecake! We'll be laughing all the way to the bank, I tell you!"

I scratched my whiskers. Writing a book is a lot of work. I wanted to think about it first. But as usual, Shif wouldn't take no for an answer. He began spouting dates and schedules. "Let's see, we'll bring it out for the Christmas season. That means I'll need your manuscript by next week, or maybe tomorrow, or maybe **today**."

He jumped up, clapping his paws. "Well, what are you waiting for, Stilton? **Get moving, moving, moving!!!**"

he squeaked.

The others all agreed. I tried to argue, but Shif locked me in my office. I was stuck typing away at my computer all day and all night!

Are you curious about how it all ended? I finished the book in a jiffy. Two months later, it was turned into a movie script. When the movie was released, it broke all box office records. Yes, I am happy to squeak, it was

A FABUMOUSE SUCCESS!

ABOUT THE AUTHOR

Born in New Mouse City, Mouse Island, Geronimo Stilton is Rattus Emeritus of Mousomorphic Literature and of Neo-Ratonic Comparative Philosophy. For the past twenty years, he has been running *The Rodent's Gazette*, New Mouse City's most widely read daily newspaper.

Stilton was awarded the Ratitzer Prize for his scoop on *The Curse of the Cheese Pyramid*. He has also received the Andersen 2000 Prize for Personality of the Year. One of his bestsellers won the 2002 eBook Award for world's best ratlings' electronic book. His works have been published all over the globe.

In his spare time, Mr. Stilton collects antique cheese rinds and plays golf. But what he most enjoys is telling stories to his nephew Benjamin.

Want to read my next adventure?
It's sure to be a fur-raising experience!

THE WILD, WILD WEST

Rat-munching rattlesnakes, was I excited! I was on a wagon train to the wild, wild West. But before you could say "hi-ho, cowboy," I found myself in a showdown with the wickedest rat in all of Cactus City. All I wanted was to ride off into the sunset with the wind in my whiskers . . . but it looked like I'd be lucky to escape with my tail!

Don't miss any of my other fabumouse adventures!

#1 Lost Treasure of the Emerald Eye

#2 The Curse of the Cheese Pyramid

#3 Cat and Mouse in a Haunted House

#4 I'm Too Fond of My Fur!

#5 Four Mice Deep in the Jungle

#6 Paws Off, Cheddarface!

#7 Red Pizzas for a Blue Count

#8 Attack of the Bandit Cats

Don't miss any of my other fabumouse adventures!

#1 Lost Treasure of the Emerald Eye
#2 The Curse of the Cheese Pyramid
#3 Cat and Mouse in a Haunted House
#4 I'm Too Fond of My Fur!
#5 Four Mice Deep in the Jungle
#6 Paws Off, Cheddarface!
#7 Red Pizzas for a Blue Count
#8 Attack of the Bandit Cats
#9 A Fabumouse Vacation for Geronimo
#10 All Because of a Cup of Coffee
#11 It's Halloween, You 'Fraidy Mouse!
#12 Merry Christmas, Geronimo!
#13 The Phantom of the Subway
#14 The Temple of the Ruby of Fire
#15 The Mona Mousa Code
#16 A Cheese-Colored Camper
#17 Watch Your Whiskers, Stilton!
#18 Shipwreck on the Pirate Islands
#19 My Name is Stilton, Geronimo Stilton
#20 Surf's Up, Geronimo!
#21 The Wild, Wild West
#22 The Secret of Cacklefur Castle
#23 Valentine's Day Disaster
#24 Field Trip to Niagara Falls

#25 The Search for Sunken Treasure
#26 The Mummy With No Name
#27 The Christmas Toy Factory
#28 Wedding Crasher
#29 Down and Out Down Under
#30 The Mouse Island Marathon
#31 The Mysterious Cheese Thief
#32 Valley of the Giant Skeletons
#33 Geronimo and the Gold Medal Mystery
#34 Geronimo Stilton, Secret Agent
#35 A Very Merry Christmas
#36 Geronimo's Valentine
#37 The Race Across America
#38 A Fabumouse School Adventure
#39 Singing Sensation
#40 The Karate Mouse
#41 Mighty Mount Kilimanjaro
#42 The Peculiar Pumpkin Thief
#43 I'm Not a Supermouse!
#44 The Giant Diamond Robbery
#45 The Haunted Castle
A Christmas Tale
Christmas Catastrophe

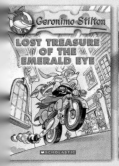

Be sure to check out these very special editions!

THE KINGDOM OF FANTASY

THE QUEST FOR PARADISE: THE RETURN TO THE KINGDOM OF FANTASY

And look for this new series about my friend Creepella von Cacklefur!

#1 THE THIRTEEN GHOSTS

#2 MEET ME IN HORRORWOOD

If you like my brother's books, you'll love mine!

THEA STILTON AND THE DRAGON'S CODE

THEA STILTON AND THE MOUNTAIN OF FIRE

THEA STILTON AND THE GHOST OF THE SHIPWRECK

THEA STILTON AND THE SECRET CITY

THEA STILTON AND THE MYSTERY IN PARIS

THEA STILTON AND THE CHERRY BLOSSOM ADVENTURE

THEA STILTON AND THE STAR CASTAWAYS

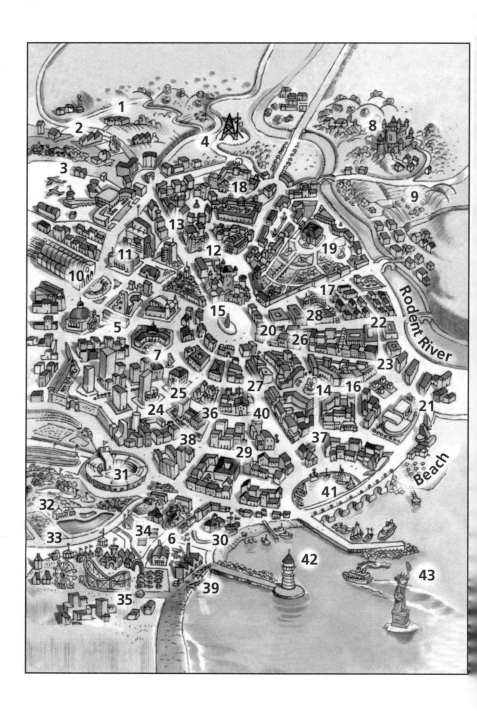

Rodent River

Beach

Map of New Mouse City

1. Industrial Zone
2. Cheese Factories
3. Angorat International Airport
4. WRAT Radio and Television Station
5. Cheese Market
6. Fish Market
7. Town Hall
8. Snotnose Castle
9. The Seven Hills of Mouse Island
10. Mouse Central Station
11. Trade Center
12. Movie Theater
13. Gym
14. Catnegie Hall
15. Singing Stone Plaza
16. The Gouda Theater
17. Grand Hotel
18. Mouse General Hospital
19. Botanical Gardens
20. Cheap Junk for Less (Trap's store)
21. Parking Lot
22. Mouseum of Modern Art
23. University and Library
24. *The Daily Rat*
25. *The Rodent's Gazette*
26. Trap's House
27. Fashion District
28. The Mouse House Restaurant
29. Environmental Protection Center
30. Harbor Office
31. Mousidon Square Garden
32. Golf Course
33. Swimming Pool
34. Blushing Meadow Tennis Courts
35. Curlyfur Island Amusement Park
36. Geronimo's House
37. New Mouse City Historic District
38. Public Library
39. Shipyard
40. Thea's House
41. New Mouse Harbor
42. Luna Lighthouse
43. The Statue of Liberty

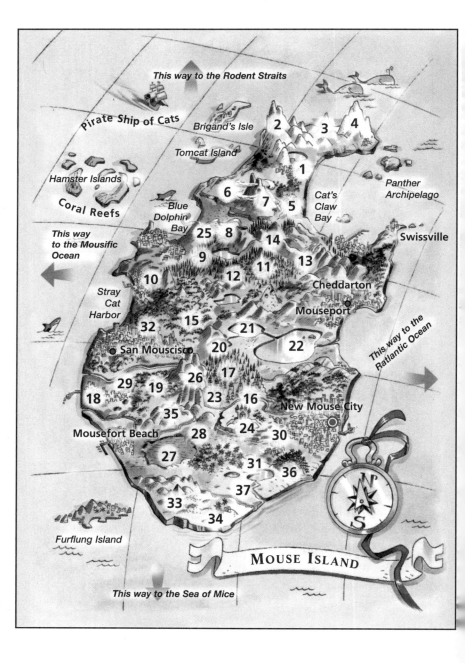

Map of Mouse Island

1. Big Ice Lake
2. Frozen Fur Peak
3. Slipperyslopes Glacier
4. Coldcreeps Peak
5. Ratzikistan
6. Transratania
7. Mount Vamp
8. Roastedrat Volcano
9. Brimstone Lake
10. Poopedcat Pass
11. Stinko Peak
12. Dark Forest
13. Vain Vampires Valley
14. Goose Bumps Gorge
15. The Shadow Line Pass
16. Penny Pincher Lodge
17. Nature Reserve Park
18. Las Ratayas Marinas
19. Fossil Forest
20. Lake Lake

21. Lake Lake Lake
22. Lake Lakelakelake
23. Cheddar Crag
24. Cannycat Castle
25. Valley of the Giant Sequoia
26. Cheddar Springs
27. Sulfurous Swamp
28. Old Reliable Geyser
29. Vole Vail
30. Ravingrat Ravine
31. Gnat Marshes
32. Munster Highlands
33. Mousehara Desert
34. Oasis of the Sweaty Camel
35. Cabbagehead Hill
36. Rattytrap Jungle
37. Rio Mosquito

Dear mouse friends,
Thanks for reading, and farewell
till the next book.
It'll be another whisker-licking-good
adventure, and that's a promise!

Geronimo Stilton